Hardback ISBN: 979-8-9869091-1-0
Paperback ISBN: 979-8-9869091-5-8
eBook ISBN: 979-8-9869091-9-6

Published by Nicely Publishing

Printed in the United States

www.ezerthebagel.com
hello@ezerthebagel.com
@ezerthebagel

1/2 Basset + 1/2 Beagle

= Ezer the Bagel

WOOF!
WOOF!

TREATS

EZER

Mr. Birdie, the neighborhood Friend Coach, is VERY wise and knows everything about friendships!

He says being a good friend is about always choosing to be the best we can be for one another.

My friend, Francie, tends to eat worms, so I gently remind her that cookies are much better.

I tend to act like a pig and scarf up too many treats, so Francie reminds me to slow down and really enjoy my food.

My friend, Theodore, tends to be a little rough when meeting new doggies, so I remind him to say "Hello" nicely.

I tend to get distracted and wander off, and Theodore herds me back to the group so I don't get lost.

I tend to be a lazy couch potato, and Macan uses his cheerful energy to encourage me to get up and play.

I tend to slouch and not pay attention, so Cerra reminds me to sit up straight and be aware of my surroundings.

My friend, Mishka, tends to beg when our humans are eating, so I remind him to wait patiently.

I tend to run across the street without looking, so Mishka reminds me to look both ways before crossing.

My friend, Koko, tends to jump on me, so I remind him with a loving and stern look that it bothers me.

I tend to pull too hard on walks, so Koko reminds me to slow down and take it easy.

My friends, Nika and Woody, are siblings. Nika likes to speak up when she has something to say.

Woody is SUPER strong and encourages me to stand up for myself.

Honest Capable Important Smart Beautiful
Dishonest Incapable Useless Stupid Ugly

"Choose to **forgive** easily instead of holding grudges..."

"Always remember that choosing to be the best we can be for one another, will help our friendships grow

This book is dedicated to my favorite human.

She takes me on the best walks, gives me the best treats, listens to my stories, takes selfies with me, and tells me that I'm a gorgeous boy.

Thank you for always taking good care of me.

Wove you to the moon and back, Michellie!

In addition to raising two amazing children, Marisa Nicely has been an educator for more than thirty years. Passionate about helping kids discover their personal value, strengths, and potential, she has noticed that it seems to be more and more challenging for children to walk in the confidence of who they were created to be.

When she found her Basset/Beagle, he inspired the children around her with so much joy and love, she decided to write an entire book series about him. Ezer the Bagel is an excellent resource that partners with parents by teaching children life skills that really matter, such as self-worth, awareness of self and others, resilience, courage, purpose, and more!

Learn more about the Ezer the Bagel series at
www.EzerTheBagel.com

1/2 Basset + 1/2 Beagle

= Ezer the Bagel

I don't know about you, but my friends are very important to me. Yip, yip!

Mr. Birdie, the neighborhood Friend Coach, is VERY wise and knows everything about friendships!

He says being a good friend is about
always choosing to be the best
we can be for one another.

My friend, Francie, tends to eat worms, so I gently remind her that cookies are much better.

I tend to act like a pig and scarf up too many treats, so Francie reminds me to slow down and really enjoy my food.

My friend, Theodore, tends to be a little rough when meeting new doggies, so I remind him to say "Hello" nicely.

I tend to get distracted and wander
off, and Theodore herds me back
to the group so I don't get lost.

My friend, Macan, is HUGE and tends to be bouncy, so I remind him to settle down—especially in the car!

I tend to be a lazy couch potato, and Macan uses his cheerful energy to encourage me to get up and play.

I tend to run across the street without looking, so Mishka reminds me to look both ways before crossing.

My friend, Koko, tends to jump on me, so I remind him with a loving and stern look that it bothers me.

I tend to pull too hard on walks, so Koko reminds me to slow down and take it easy.

My friends, Nika and Woody, are siblings. Nika likes to speak up when she has something to say.

Woody is SUPER strong and encourages me to stand up for myself.

Honest Capable Important Smart Beautiful

Dishonest Incapable Useless Stupid Ugly

"Choose to **forgive** easily instead of holding grudges..."

"Always remember that choosing to be the best we can be for one another, will help our friendships grow

This book is dedicated to my favorite human.

She takes me on the best walks, gives me the best treats, listens to my stories, takes selfies with me, and tells me that I'm a gorgeous boy.

Thank you for always taking good care of me.

Wove you to the moon and back, Michellie!

In addition to raising two amazing children, Marisa Nicely has been an educator for more than thirty years. Passionate about helping kids discover their personal value, strengths, and potential, she has noticed that it seems to be more and more challenging for children to walk in the confidence of who they were created to be.

When she found her Basset/Beagle, he inspired the children around her with so much joy and love, she decided to write an entire book series about him. Ezer the Bagel is an excellent resource that partners with parents by teaching children life skills that really matter, such as self-worth, awareness of self and others, resilience, courage, purpose, and more!

Learn more about the Ezer the Bagel series at
www.EzerTheBagel.com

Printed in the USA
CPSIA information can be obtained
at www.ICGtesting.com
JSHW040457051223
53245JS00001B/1